Zac's Freaky Frogs
published in 2009 by
Hardie Grant Egmont
Ground Floor, Building 1, 658 Church Street
Richmond, Victoria 3121, Australia
www.hardiegrantegmont.com.au

PEFC
PEFC/21-31-16

*The pages of this book are printed on paper derived
from forests promoting sustainable management.*

A CiP record for this title is available from the National Library of Australia

Printed in Australia by McPherson's Printing Group

3 5 7 9 10 8 6 4

ZAC'S FREAKY FROGS

BY H. I. LARRY

ILLUSTRATIONS BY ANDY HOOK, RON MONNIER & ASH OSWALD

hardie grant EGMONT

CHAPTER... ...ONE

Zac Power was in the school gym. He was playing a game of basketball. His team was winning.

Zac caught the ball
and threw it. It went
straight into the hoop.

 **'Go, team!'**
Zac yelled.

Zac was 12 years old.
He was a spy who went
on cool missions. Being
a spy was top secret.

Only Zac's family knew he was a spy. Zac's mum and dad were spies, too. So was his brother, Leon.

Zac's family were part of the spy group called GIB. They worked to stop an evil spy group called BIG.

All GIB spies had code names. Zac's was Agent Rock Star.

AGENT / ZAC POWER
CODE NAME / AGENT ROCK STAR
AGE / 12

IDENTITY TOP SECRET

GOVERNMENT
G★I★B
INVESTIGATION BUREAU

His brother Leon's code name was Agent Tech Head.

Leon was in charge
of the GIB Test Labs.
Leon made cool
gadgets. And Zac got
to test drive them.

Zac looked at his watch.
The basketball game
was nearly over.
Zac looked up at the
scoreboard.

The score was 30 to 28. Then the numbers on the board started to flash.

Zac blinked. *It's a secret message*, he thought. *It has to be.*

The scoreboard was flashing GIB.

Zac looked around.
He was the only
one looking at the
scoreboard.

CHAPTER... ...TWO

Zac waved at his coach.
He had to stop playing.
Zac asked his coach
if he could leave.
As Zac walked off,

he looked up at the
scoreboard again.

14:51

GO TO THE
LOCKER ROOM

Zac went to the locker
room. *Now what do
I do?* he thought.

He walked over to his locker and opened the door. *There's nothing here,* thought Zac. *Weird.*

Then he saw a sign at the back of his locker. It said **Spy Hatch**.

There was a wheel under the sign.

Cool! thought Zac.
He turned the wheel.
The locker wall
opened like a door.

Wow! grinned Zac.

Zac looked through.
There was a big
blow-up tunnel slide.

A kiddie slide?
thought Zac.
*Blow-up slides are for
babies! I'm too old
for that.*

Suddenly Zac heard a
voice from inside
the slide.

'Hey, Zac! said the
voice. 'This isn't just
a blow-up slide.
It's the new *GIB Speed
of Light Flight-slide*.
Hurry up and jump
on. I need you.'

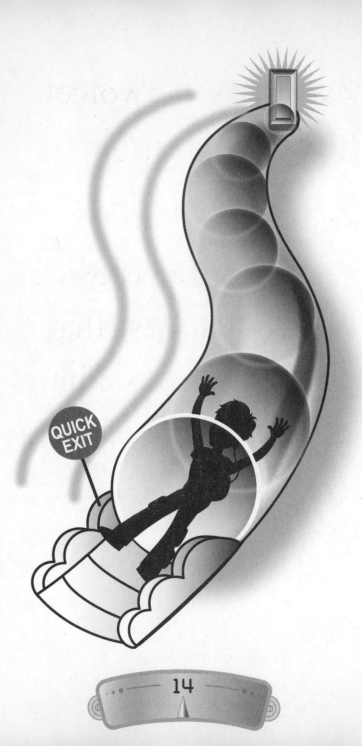

QUICK
EXIT

14

Zac knew the voice.
It was Leon's.

Zac jumped on the
slide and flew down.
He went so fast that
everything was a blur!
Zac stood up. He was
in a GIB Test Lab.

CHAPTER... ...THREE

'What took you so long?' Leon asked.

'We were winning basketball!' grumbled Zac.

'Well, I need you to do some test driving, Zac,' said Leon. 'This is my latest spy vehicle. It's called the Triox.

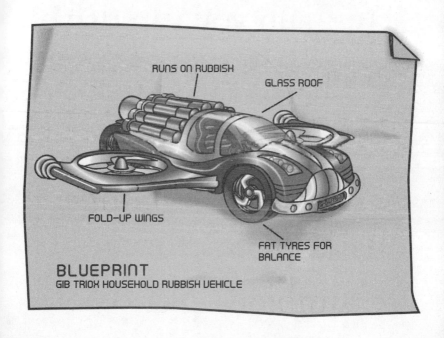

RUNS ON RUBBISH

GLASS ROOF

FOLD–UP WINGS

FAT TYRES FOR BALANCE

BLUEPRINT
GIB TRIOX HOUSEHOLD RUBBISH VEHICLE

It runs on rubbish, so it sort of recycles things.'

Zac laughed. 'It uses rubbish to make it go?'

'Yes, and you can drive or fly it,' said Leon. 'It goes super-fast!'

Zac looked at the Triox. It had three wheels and a glass roof.

It looked like a cross
between a plane
and a car. Zac got
into the driver's seat.

'Check out the pair
of pants on the seat,'
said Leon.

The pants were pink
and had huge gold
flowers on them.

'Gross! said Zac. 'I'm not wearing those!'

'The pants need testing, too,' grinned Leon. 'Turn them over.'

Zac pulled an ugly face at Leon.

Then Zac turned the pants over. There was a small label on the back.

PARACHUTE PANTS

PULL CORD TO OPEN PARACHUTE

'Good idea, Leon,' said Zac. 'But they are SO not cool!'

Leon was such a geek!

'These are very cool, Zac,' said Leon. 'When you pull the cord, the pants turn into a parachute.'

Zac got out of the Triox.

He put the parachute pants on over his jeans.

They were huge. Zac thought he looked really bad.

Zac groaned. He got back into the Triox.

Suddenly the control panel flashed with a message.

> MISSION FOR
> AGENT ROCK STAR.
> PLEASE CHECK YOUR SPYPAD.

Every spy had a SpyPad. It was a phone and a computer and could crack codes. Zac put music and games on his.

■■■■■■■■■

TOP SECRET
FOR THE EYES OF
ZAC POWER ONLY

MISSION SENT
THURSDAY 4PM

Latest spy gear to test drive:
Parachute pants and
Recycling Triox.

BIG has let poisonous frogs
loose on Poison Island.
They must be removed.
Take a can of Frog Fix
to Agent Toad Rage.

END

Zac took out his SpyPad and his mission popped up.

'You should go,' said Leon. 'When I push this button the lab roof will open. Fly the Triox through the gap in the roof.'

The roof slid open a little bit. Zac looked up at the space. 'You must be joking!' said Zac. 'That space is too small.'

'Push the Wings Up button,' called Leon. 'Then the wings will go straight up.'

Zac pushed the button and the wings went up.

He pulled on the Triox's joystick.

Zac waved to Leon and flew up through the gap in the roof.

'Don't forget to do
your test drive
report!' called Leon.

CHAPTER... ...FOUR

Zac sat back and checked out the Triox's control panel.

How do I get to Poison Island? thought Zac.

Then he saw
a button.

Excellent,
thought Zac.
*A machine that can fly
by itself!* He set the
auto pilot and then
looked around.

Zac found a pizza
maker. *Awesome!*

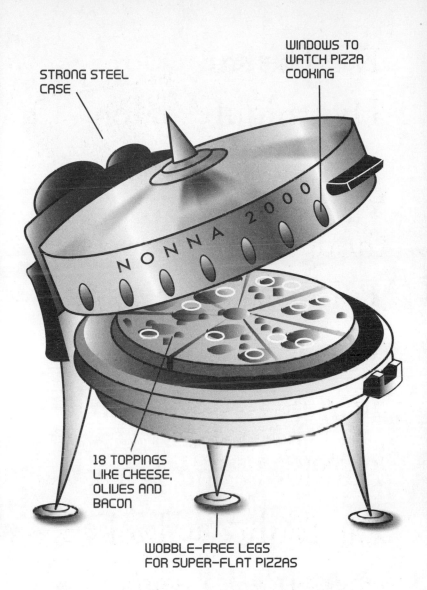

STRONG STEEL
CASE

WINDOWS TO
WATCH PIZZA
COOKING

NONNA 2000

18 TOPPINGS
LIKE CHEESE,
OLIVES AND
BACON

WOBBLE-FREE LEGS
FOR SUPER-FLAT PIZZAS

33

Zac turned it on.
Five minutes later,
he was eating his
favourite pizza.

Poison Island was just
up ahead. *It won't be
long now*, thought Zac.

Suddenly the Triox
stopped. Zac looked
at its power-maker.

It needed
more rubbish.

Zac grabbed all the
rubbish from the bin.
He pushed it into
the power-maker.
The Triox started
moving again.

Phew! thought Zac.
That was close.

But then the Triox
stopped again.

Oh, no! thought Zac.
*I don't have any more
rubbish.*

Then Zac remembered
his parachute pants.

Of course, he thought.
I can jump out of the
Triox. I'll float down
to the island using
the parachute.

But how would Zac
get back to the Triox?

Then he saw a button
on the control panel.

*It must send the Triox
back to GIB*, thought
Zac. He pushed the
button and jumped
out of the Triox.

CHAPTER... ...FIVE

Zac was falling fast.
His pants were
flapping in the air.
Zac pulled on the cord
but nothing happened.

He pulled the cord
again. He tugged
and tugged. Still
nothing happened!
Zac pulled as hard as
he could. Finally it
worked.

Zac's pants puffed
up into a big pink
and gold parachute.

The parachute made
Zac hang upside down!
Not my best spy moment,
thought Zac.

Zac hit the ground
and rolled a few times
before he stopped.
That was when he
felt something in
his pocket.

He looked in the
pocket of his pants.
There was a can
of Frog Fix.

Zac stood up and his pants went down to normal size. *Amazing*, thought Zac.

Then he looked at the hill in front of him. There were frogs coming from everywhere. Frogs filled with poison!

Zac had never seen
so many frogs.

They were big and
super slimy-looking.

Zac started to spray
them with the Frog Fix.

It made the frogs roll
up into little balls.
Then they rolled down
the hill into the sea.

Zac had to jump over the frogs as they rolled. He knew he could still be poisoned if he touched them.

I need to find Agent Toad Rage, thought Zac. He saw him standing at the top of the hill. Agent Toad Rage was waving.

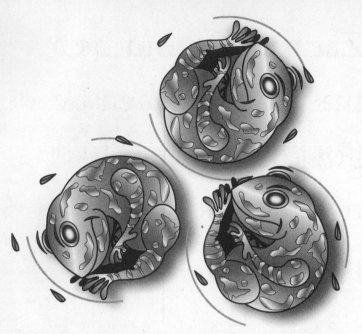

Zac began to run up
the hill. He sprayed
more frogs. They rolled
down and he jumped
over them.

Zac was fit, but he was puffed when he got to the top. He'd never done so much jumping.

'Well done,' said Agent Toad Rage. 'You got rid of all the frogs.'

'Yes,' puffed Zac. 'And here is the Frog Fix.'

He gave the can
to Agent Toad Rage.

'Thanks,' said Agent
Toad Rage. 'You
should go back to GIB.'

CHAPTER... ...SIX

Agent Toad Rage
pointed to the other
side of the island.
'If you go that way
GIB will pick you up.'

'Excellent,' said Zac. 'But what about BIG? They put the frogs here!'

'BIG got away,' said Agent Toad Rage. 'Those pants you're wearing must have scared them off!'

'Yeah!' grinned Zac.

'They scared me at first, too. They're really ugly. But they work well.'

Zac started walking down the hill. When he got to the beach he sat down under a tree and waited for GIB to pick him up.

Zac took out his SpyPad. He wanted to play his favourite game. But a message popped up. It was from Leon.

Good job. Do your test drive report before you play silly games.

You are such a pain, Leon! groaned Zac. *Well, the gross-looking parachute pants saved me. But the Triox used up too much rubbish.*

He began to fill out his report.

TEST DRIVE
REPORT
TRIOX HOUSEHOLD
RUBBISH VEHICLE
Rating:

The Triox could fly really well.
But it ate all the rubbish too quickly.

PARACHUTE PANTS
Rating:

These pants are really ugly!
But they did everything I wanted.
Thank you, Leon!

END

... THE END ...